On the Way to the Pond

P9-EMC-898

On the

Way to the Pond

Angela Shelf Medearis

Illustrated by Lorinda Bryan Cauley

Green Light Readers
Harcourt, Inc.

Orlando Austin New York San Diego Toronto London

One day, Tess Tiger went to visit Herbert Hippo. They were hungry. Herbert packed a big basket for a picnic at the pond. It was full of good food.

"You bring the lunch," said Tess. "I'll bring these four very important things."
Herbert looked at them and just nodded.

They started up the path. It was a very hot day. All of a sudden, Herbert felt sick.

"Sit under my umbrella," said Tess.
"I'll fan you."
"Thanks," said Herbert.

When Herbert felt better, they went off to the pond. All of a sudden, Herbert stopped and cried, "Oh no! I forgot the basket!"

"I'll go back and get it," said Tess. "You go on."

Tess dropped some rocks as she walked. She found the picnic basket and turned to go back.

On the way, Tess stopped. First she looked this way. Then she looked that way. She was lost!

"It's a good thing I dropped these rocks," she said. "I'll just follow them back."

Tess got to the pond, but she couldn't find Herbert. "Oh no! Herbert is lost!" She got out her whistle. *R-r-r-r-r-r!*

"Here I am!" cried Herbert.
"I'm glad you had all that important stuff!"

"Yes," said Tess, "and I'm glad you packed a big lunch! I'm starving!"

I Can Do This!

Tess Tiger and Herbert Hippo are good friends. They like to do things together. Make a book to show what special things you can do with your family and friends.

WHAT YOU'LL NEED

paper   **crayons or markers**

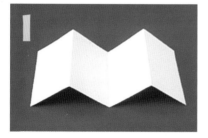

1 Fold a big sheet of paper to make an accordion book.

Make a cover.

Draw pictures of things you can do with your family and friends.

Share your book with a group.

Make a Picnic Snack

Herbert packed lots of good food for his picnic with Tess. If you go on a picnic, bring along this tasty snack!

WHAT YOU'LL NEED

pretzels   **raisins**   **popcorn**   **nuts**

small plastic
bags

measuring
cup

large self-closing
plastic bags

3 cups popcorn

1 cup nuts

2 cups pretzels

2 cups raisins

- Measure each ingredient and pour them into a large plastic bag.

- Close the bag. Shake the bag to mix up your snack.

- Pour or scoop out the snack into small bags.

Now you and your friends
have a delicious

picnic snack!

Meet the Author and Illustrator

Angela Shelf Medearis loves to laugh and write silly stories. She has an office filled with toys. The toys give her ideas and make her laugh. She hopes that *On the Way to the Pond* puts a smile on your face.

Angela Shelf Medearis

It takes Lorinda Bryan Cauley about four days to draw the picture for one page of a book. First she does pencil drawings. Then she adds color with colored pencils and colored ink. Lorinda works very hard on the characters' eyes. She thinks the eyes are very important for showing feelings. What do you think?

Lorinda Bryan Cauley